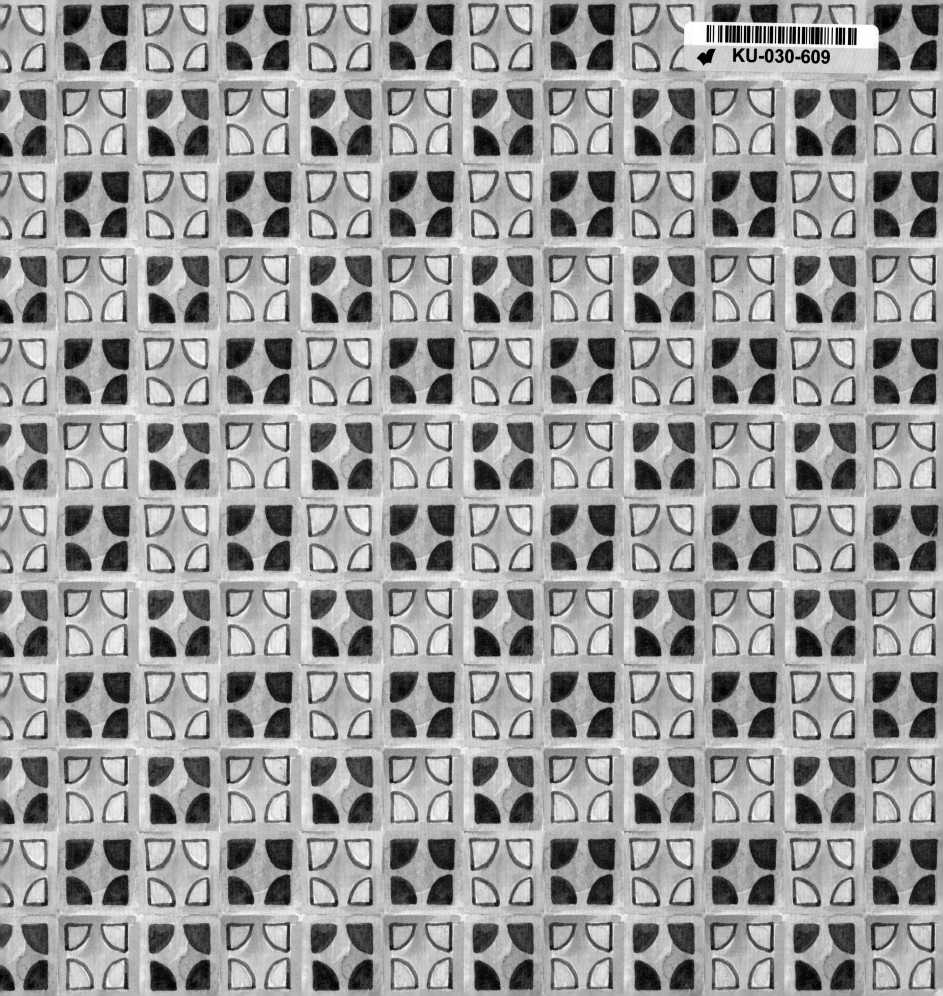

For
Grandad Burns and Grandad Roberts
and to the memory of
Nana Jean Burns and
Grandma Anne "Queenie" Roberts

First published in Great Britain in 2003

This paperback edition first published in Great Britain in 2004 by
Chrysalis Children's Books,
an imprint of Chrysalis Books Group plc
The Chrysalis Building, Bramley Road,
London W10 6SP
www.chrysalisbooks.co.uk

Text © Lynn Roberts 2003
Illustrations © David Roberts 2003
Design and layout © Breslich & Foss Ltd.

The moral right of the author and illustrator has been asserted

A CIP catalogue record for this book is available from the British Library.

ISBN 1 84458 156 X

Set in Simoncini Garamond

Printed in China

2 4 6 8 10 9 7 5 3 1

This book can be ordered direct from the publisher. Please contact
the Marketing Department. But try your bookshop first.

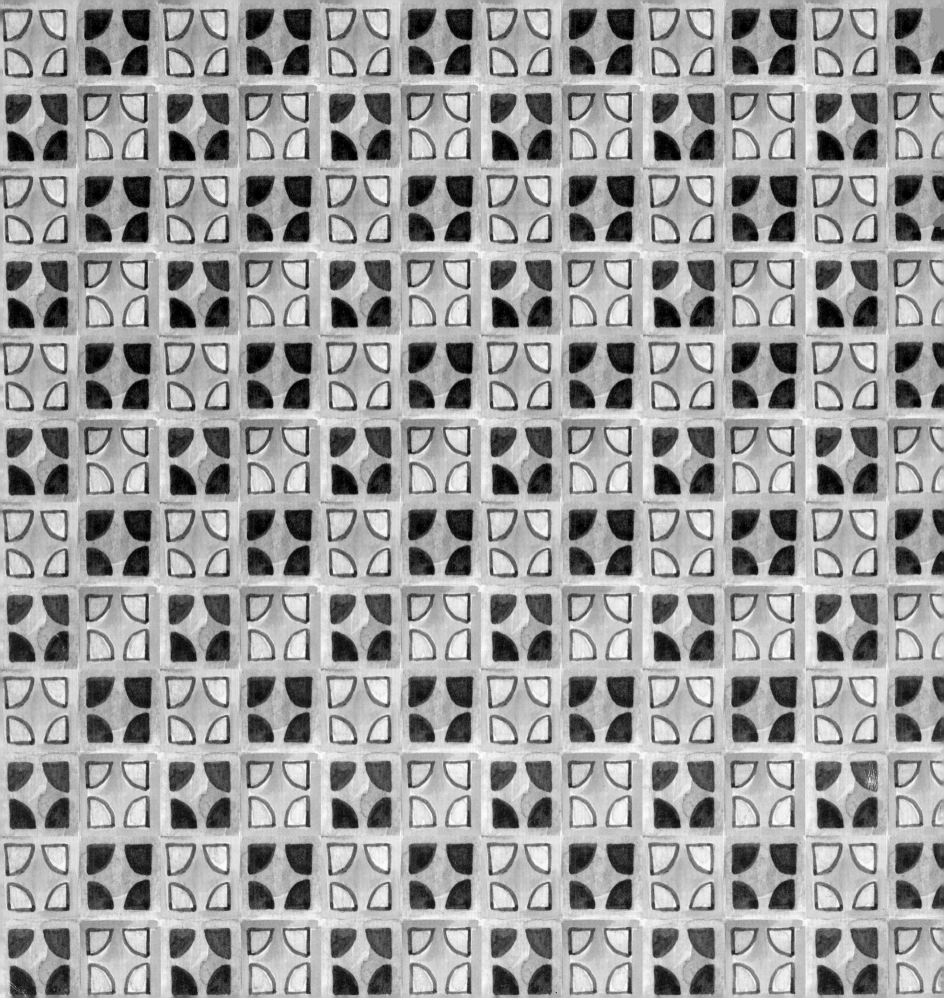

Rapunzel

a groovy
fairy tale

RETOLD BY
Lynn Roberts

ILLUSTRATED BY
David Roberts

Chrysalis Children's Books

In a time not too long ago and in a land much like our own, there lived a very beautiful girl with the most extraordinarily long red hair.

Her name was Rapunzel and she lived with her Aunt Edna and Roach, Edna's hideous pet crow. Rapunzel had been brought up by Edna after her parents died when she was very young. Edna kept her locked up so she could not go out and enjoy herself.

To keep Rapunzel quiet (and to make herself seem nice, which she was not) Edna brought Rapunzel second-hand magazines and records and occasionally allowed her to watch television. "When you are older," Edna lied, "I'll take you out and show you the city, but it's not safe for you on your own."

Rapunzel believed every word, for she knew nothing of the world.

The tower block they lived in was old and deserted. The lift was always broken and there were hundreds of stairs to the ground. This was not a problem for Aunt Edna as she had a special way of entering and leaving the building.

Rapunzel would hang her plait over the balcony and Edna would climb down it. On her return she would shout, "Rapunzel, Rapunzel, let down your hair!" Then, Rapunzel would throw her long plait over the balcony, Edna would grab hold, and Rapunzel would slowly pull her up.

Aunt Edna worked at the local school. She was the most fearsome dinner lady the children had ever seen. Prowling around the canteen, she would force them to eat every scrap of food, even cold pea soup and lumpy custard. Edna also trained Roach to swoop down and steal things from the children to bring to her. Edna selfishly took all the best things and gave the scarves and jewellery she didn't like to Rapunzel, pretending she had bought them.

One morning, as Aunt Edna struggled down Rapunzel's hair,

a boy who had stopped to fix his bike on the way to school

happened to see this extraordinary sight. His name was Roger and he

was the singer in the local school band, Roger and the Rascals.

Intrigued, he thought, "Surely that's the nasty dinner lady from school!

What is she doing?"

After school, he raced back to the tower block. To his astonishment,

he heard the nasty dinner lady booming

out, "Rapunzel, Rapunzel, let down

your hair!" Seeing the beautiful

red plait tumble over the

balcony, Roger knew he had to

meet the girl with the long hair.

The next day was Saturday, and Roger could not wait to go back.
Luckily for him, Edna was just on her way to a much-needed fitness class.

Roger took a deep breath and, trying his best to imitate Edna's
booming voice, he called, "Rapunzel, Rapunzel, let down your hair!"
To his amazement, the rope of hair was lowered. Hesitantly Roger took
hold of it, then gasped as he was lifted into the air.

As he reached the balcony, he fell over the wall onto all fours.

"Oh my!" Rapunzel exclaimed as she found herself face to face with
the most handsome boy she had ever seen.

Rapunzel and Roger spent the whole morning listening to music and talking.

"I feel as if I've known you forever," Rapunzel cried, gazing into Roger's eyes.

Every day after this, Roger would wait for Edna to leave and then visit Rapunzel to say good morning before he went to school. He took Rapunzel a present every lunch time, and sometimes he took along his guitar so he could sing his new songs for her. She was happier than she had ever been.

One day, Roger said, "I wish I could find a way to get you out of the flat so that I could show you the city. You can't very well climb down your own hair, and we cannot take the stairs as Edna never forgets to lock the door."

Rapunzel thought for a moment. "I've got a great idea!" she said. "Why don't we make a rope ladder from all the scarves and belts I have?"

Together they set to work.

The very next day, after saying goodbye to Roger, Rapunzel let her hair down for her aunt. As Edna reached the top, Rapunzel said without thinking, "You are so heavy, Aunt. It is so much easier to pull up my dear Roger."

The moment the words were out, Rapunzel knew she had spoiled everything.

Edna flew into a rage. She grabbed a pair of scissors and cut off Rapunzel's long hair. "How dare you deceive me?" cried Edna as she forced Rapunzel to climb down her own hair. "May you never find happiness!" she screamed. Seething with anger, Edna waited on the balcony for Roger.

Before long, Roger called to Rapunzel to let down her hair and whistled as he was lifted up, happy at the thought of seeing her again.

But to his horror, when he reached the top, the ugly, twisted face of Edna leered out at him.

"You will never see Rapunzel again," Edna hissed in his ear as she pushed him backwards over the balcony. The hair tumbled with him as he fell to the ground. Wrapped around him, the plait broke his fall, but he banged his head and fell unconscious.

Meanwhile, wandering through the city streets, Rapunzel grew tired and hungry. She found a stray kitten nearly as hungry as she was and called him Rascal after Roger's band. All her life she had wanted to visit the city, but never had she felt more lonely and lost. "Will I ever see Roger again?" she wondered, holding Rascal close.

Roger, however, remembered nothing about Rapunzel. Dazed from his fall, he staggered home with the hair he had found wrapped around his body. He truly had no idea where it had come from. He put it in his dad's garage which he used as a studio. "It must mean something," he puzzled as he practised his guitar.

Rapunzel slept in a damp shop doorway that night, with Rascal clasped in her arms. As she awoke, stretching her arms and yawning, she caught sight of a poster. "Roger!" she cried out in surprise. Her beloved Roger and his band were playing a concert at the school that very evening. She would find the school and see Roger again!

Rapunzel could barely contain her excitement when she arrived for the concert. She found a space in the front row just as Roger and his band walked on stage to loud applause. Roger looked out into the crowd and, as he began to sing, his eyes rested on a strangely familiar halo of red hair. And when he looked at Rapunzel's beautiful smiling face, he remembered everything.

Rapunzel and Roger were best friends from that moment on, and as happy as could be. Roger and the Rascals became very successful, playing at every school in town. Rapunzel, deciding to make use of her glorious red hair, learned how to make wigs. She designed them in every style and length imaginable, as long as they were red!

And what happened to Aunt Edna? Well, she no longer had

Rapunzel's hair, and the lift was, of course, out of order...

Illustrator's Note

When I was asked to illustrate a second fairy tale (my first being *Cinderella: An Art Deco Love Story*),
I was very keen to use the story of Rapunzel. At my sister's suggestion, I decided to set the story in a 1970s
tower block, the obvious association with the 1970s being Rapunzel's long hair. As a child growing up at that
time, I was very influenced by the music, films, fashion and design of the period. In researching this book,
I looked at old family photos and magazines to help me remember the clothes and toys I had owned as a child.
I have incorporated record sleeves, film posters, furniture and product design from this period into my
illustrations. I also wanted to link Cinderella to Rapunzel in a subtle way. I imagined the families to be related,
and so a few artefacts from *Cinderella* have been passed down and found their way into Rapunzel's home.

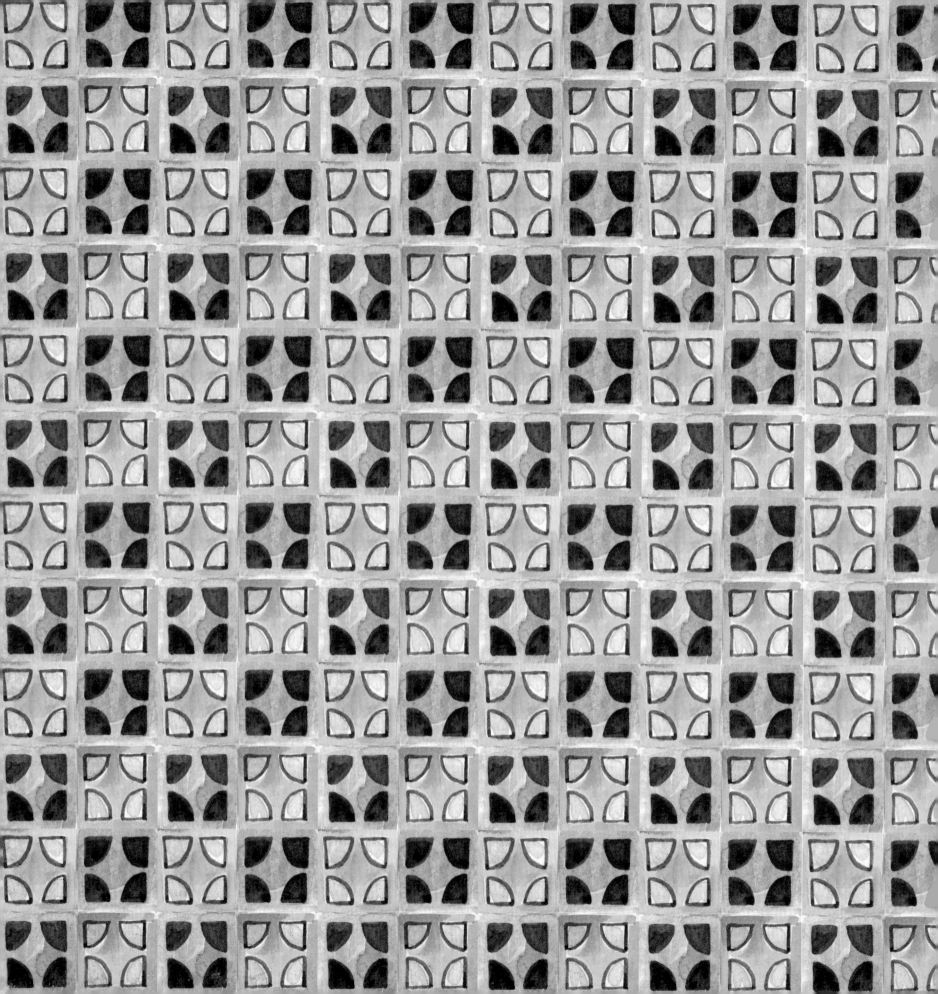

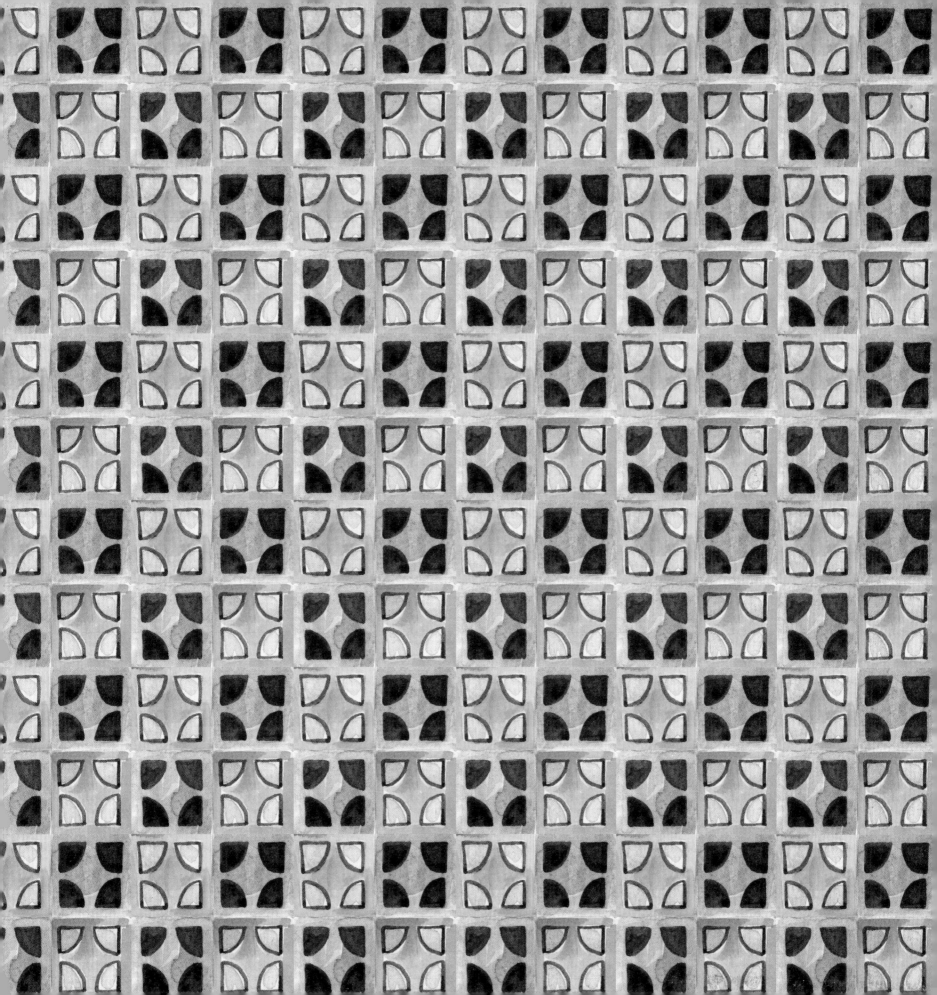